BEAUTY
AND THE BEAST

A long time ago and far away, there lived a wealthy merchant and his three daughters. The older girls were proud and selfish, while the youngest girl was as generous and kind as she was beautiful.

One day, the merchant heard that all his ships had been lost in a storm. He was penniless and would have to move to a tiny cottage on the edge of the woods.

"Everything will be alright," said the youngest daughter, Beauty. "We can all help. We don't need any servants as the house is so small."

The merchant was very grateful to Beauty. The older girls were very upset, and were no help at all.

In no time at all, Beauty had the little cottage spick and span.

One day, a messenger arrived.

"I have good news," he said to the merchant. "One of your ships has made harbour. You are needed to oversee matters in the unloading."

"Oh, good news indeed!" said the merchant. He called his daughters around him.

They were delighted when they heard the news.

"Does this mean that we can move back home?" asked the oldest daughter.

"First things first," said her father. "If there is a profit, I'll bring you all back a present. You must tell me what you would like."

"Oh, a beautiful dress, father," cried the first.

"A new hat, father," said the second.

"And what about you, Beauty?" asked the merchant of his youngest daugher. Beauty simply said, "A red rose please, father."

The merchant set out that very day for the town with the messenger. He completed his business, and found that he had indeed made a profit. There was enough to buy his daughters' presents and some to invest. The dress and hat were soon bought, but there were no roses to be had in the town.

It was evening when he set out for home. "Maybe I'll be able to find one on the way home," he said to himself.

He was still far from home when it started to grow dark. He was in an unfamiliar part of the forest, and knew that he would soon be lost if he did not find somewhere for the night. He suddenly saw some lights and soon found himself outside a vast mansion.

"I did not know that this was here," said the merchant. "I really must be lost!"

The merchant went into the house as the front door was open. He looked around, but there was nobody to be seen. He suddenly sniffed the air. He could smell delicious food. A table in the dining room was laid for one, so he sat and ate a hearty supper.

He suddenly remembered his horse, and went to stable it for the night, but it had already been done, and the horse was tucking into a bag of oats.

8

'How strange,' thought the merchant, returning to the house. There, a bedroom had been prepared for him. He slept well and in the morning found all his clothes had been cleaned, breakfast was ready, and his horse was saddled.

At the front door, he turned to thank his unseen host, but then he saw the garden. It was full of roses – roses of every colour.

"Now I can get Beauty's present," said the merchant, and he picked a red rose.

The merchant nearly jumped out of his skin when he heard a furious roar.

"Have I not been a good host?" roared the voice. "I fed you, gave you a bed for the night and stabled your

horse, and you repay me by stealing from me."

The owner of the voice then came into sight. The merchant shuddered. It was the ugliest creature he had ever seen.

"I am very sorry," said the merchant. "I picked it for my daughter."

"If you wish to live, you must send the first living thing you see when you arrive home," said the Beast.

"Very well," said the merchant. He knew that his dog usually greeted him first.

He then set off for home. But to his dismay, it was Beauty who ran out of the house to greet him. The dog was lying asleep in the sun.

The other girls came out to empty the saddle bags and to see their presents. He

went quietly into the house. Beauty was worried and followed him in.

"What's wrong?" she asked.

"I must send you to the Beast's house," he said sadly, and then told Beauty what had happened.

"I will go," said Beauty. "We must keep your promise."

"But you have not seen him," said her father.

"I will still go," said Beauty softly. "He surely cannot be as ugly as you say."

But Beauty did shudder the first time she saw the Beast at the house in the middle of the forest. The Beast pretended not to notice her shudder, and showed her around the house and gardens. She had a beautiful room and lovely clothes, and he gave her a magic mirror so that she could see her family whenever she wanted to.

The Beast spent every afternoon with her, and gradually she became used to his ugly face

and looked forward to seeing him, for he was kind and gentle despite his appearance.

One afternoon the Beast said, "Beauty, do you love me?"

"Love you?" repeated Beauty. "No, but I do like you, I like you a lot."

"Never mind," said the Beast and he left her, much earlier than usual.

Beauty looked in her mirror and saw that her sister was getting ready to be married.

Beauty asked the Beast if she could go to the wedding.

The Beast agreed, and he sent her in a beautiful carriage with a lovely present.

"Don't go back to him," said her father, after the wedding. "Stay here with me, for I miss you dreadfully when you are gone."

"I must," said Beauty. "I have promised to stay."

On her return, the Beast seemed very pleased to see her, and gave her all sorts of gifts, and spent a great deal of time with her.

The next time that Beauty looked in the mirror, her other sister was preparing for her wedding.

"Please may I go?" Beauty asked the Beast. "I promise I shall return again."

Again, Beauty went with gifts for her sister's wedding.

She returned soon after the wedding, and again the Beast seemed delighted to have her back.

Beauty did not look in her mirror for a long time after that, but suddenly

remembered it one afternoon when the Beast could not join her.

What she saw made her feel quite weak. Her father was ill in bed, and there were doctors and her sisters standing around him shaking their heads.

As soon as the Beast returned, Beauty ran to him. "Please, I must go home!" she

said. "My father is very ill and I must be with him."

"Very well," said the Beast. "But please take this ring with you. If the stone is bright then I am well, but if it turns dull, I am dying."

Beauty arrived home to find her father as she had seen him.

"He's been asking for you," said her sisters.

As soon as he saw his daughter, the merchant began to improve. Autumn came and went, and the merchant begged Beauty to stay.

"I am still a little weak," he said. "And it will be winter soon. Return to the Beast in spring."

Beauty agreed, and Christmas and winter were spent at the cottage.

One day, in early spring, Beauty was sorting through some drawers and found the ring that the Beast had given her.

The stone was dull and lifeless.

"I must go back!" she cried.

She left the cottage, the carriage speeding to take her back to the Beast's mansion.

"Please don't let me

be too late," she wept. She
had grown very fond of the Beast,
and was very upset that she hadn't
looked at the ring for so long.

The carriage journey seemed to take
forever to poor Beauty, but at last it swept
into the drive and went up to the house. She leapt
out and ran into the house, but the Beast
was nowhere to be found.
She searched everywhere and called and
called, but there was no answer. "He must
be in the garden," she said to herself, and
she ran out, calling his name, with a heart
full of dread.
"Beauty," she heard his voice gently
whisper.

She found him by a great bush of red
roses, the same one from which her father
and picked the rose.

Beauty ran to him and sat down to
cradle his ugly head in her arms. She was

crying and telling him how sorry she was.

He was very weak.

"Oh, Beast," she wept. "Please don't die. I do love you!"

There was a sudden flash of light, and Beauty no longer held the Beast in her arms! She looked up and saw a handsome man standing by the rose bush.

"Where is the Beast?" she asked, looking round.

"Here," said the man. "I was the Beast and I was dying. I needed you to say that you loved me. I was under a spell cast by a wicked witch, and I needed the love of a beautiful girl to save me. Now that spell has been lifted."

Beauty was delighted, and she and the young man were soon married. They lived happily in the beautiful mansion with the rose garden, and her father came to stay with them often.

HANSEL AND GRETEL

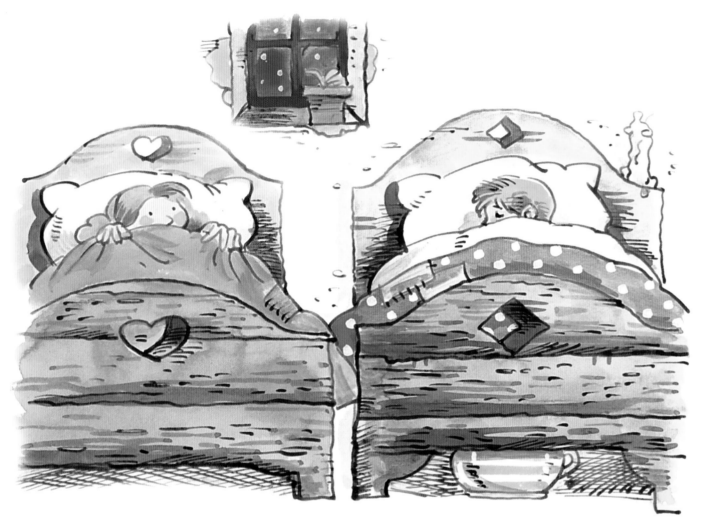

A long time ago and far away, there lived a poor woodcutter, his two children, Hansel and Gretel, and their stepmother, a selfish and unloving woman. Times were very hard indeed and the woodcutter was finding it very difficult to feed his wife and children.

One night, the woodcutter's wife spoke to him.

"Husband," she said slowly. "If the children were not here, would there be enough food for us?"

"Yes," said the woodcutter, wondering what his wife was going to say.

"If we take them into the forest," she said, "someone will probably find them."

"Are you suggesting that we just leave

them there?"
asked the
wood-cutter. "I
can't do that."

"We will
all die if we
don't do
something,"
said his wife.

"I can't do
it," said the
woodcutter, and
he turned over
and went to sleep.

Hansel had heard the whole conversation, and he was very worried.

When his father and stepmother were asleep, he crept outside and collected lots of

small white stones.

The next night the woodcutter and his wife had the same argument. Both children listened.

"What are we going to do?" Gretel whispered.

"It's alright," Hansel said. "I've already done something."

For a whole week the woman argued with the woodcutter, until finally he gave in.

"Come, children," called the stepmother early the next morning. "We're going deep into the forest for wood today, so we must be on our way."

The family set out, but Hansel seemed to be dawdling.

"Come along, Hansel," said his stepmother. "We have a long way to go."

"I'm saying goodbye to my cat," said Hansel.

"You don't have a cat," said his stepmother. "Come along."

Hansel dawdled behind for the whole journey. They went deep into the forest, much further than the children had been before and after a while they were quite lost.

They reached a clearing, and their stepmother gave them their lunch.

"Don't eat all of it now," she laughed. "Just have a short sleep. We'll be working just beyond the clearing."

The children were very tired, so they ate some of their lunch and settled down for a sleep.

They could hear their father's saw in the background and they felt quite safe.

When they awoke it was almost dark. "Father! Father!" called Hansel, hearing the sound of the saw.

The children went to look and saw that the saw had been tied to a tree, and the wind had been moving it.

"Don't worry, Gretel," said Hansel. "Just wait until the moon comes up and then we can find our way home."

Sure enough, the moonlight shone on all the little white stones that clever young Hansel had been dropping since they left the cottage. They followed the trail carefully, and by early morning they were standing outside the door of the cottage.

Their father was delighted to see them.

"How did you get so lost?" asked their stepmother, who pretended to be glad to see them. "We looked everywhere."

"We were exactly where you left us," said Gretel.

"Well, never mind, you're home safe now," said the stepmother.

The children were home, but things had not changed. There was still very little food – certainly not enough for all the family.

The stepmother nagged the woodcutter every night, saying that surely they would all starve if they did nothing, and that this time they must take the children so far into the forest that they would never find their way out again.

In despair, the woodcutter reluctantly agreed.

Again, young Hansel was listening to their conversation and when the woodcutter's wife was asleep, he went to go outside to collect more stones. But this time the door was locked and the only key was on a string around her neck. Not

knowing what to do, Hansel went silently back to bed and tried to think of a new plan.

The next morning the family left for the forest again. Instead of dropping stones, Hansel tore his bread into tiny pieces and left a trail of crumbs behind him.

They went deep into the forest. Again the children were left to sleep while their parents worked.

When they woke up, they were on their own again.

"Don't worry," said Hansel. "We'll find our way home when the moon shines."

The moon shone, but this time there was no trail to follow. All the

bread had been eaten by birds. Now the poor children were completely lost, deep in the forest and had no way of knowing which way to go.

They walked in the moonlight, and when the moon went down they found

somewhere to sleep. The next morning they walked on. As they walked, a little bird seemed to be following them. Then it chattered to them, as if telling them to follow it. The children followed the bird and they came to a clearing. In the middle was the most amazing house they had ever seen. It seemed to be made of gingerbread and marzipan, candy sticks and lumpy toffee, liquorice and jellies.

After all their walking and a night without food, the poor children were very

hungry and rushed up to it, tearing off handfuls of gingerbread and eating it.

"This is delicious!" cried Gretel, eating a piece of the roof.

"Who's that outside my door?" came a croaky voice. An old woman appeared. "Oh,

you poor children! You look so tired and hungry! Come in and have some fresh lemonade and some more to eat," she said. "And after that you must have a little rest."

"Oh, thank you, thank you!" said the grateful children, following her into the pretty little home.

But when they woke up, things were very different indeed.

Hansel found himself locked up in a cage, the gingerbread house was now a shabby, dirty cottage and the old woman was obviously a witch.

"Ha! Ha!" she shrieked. "Children – just what I like to eat! But you're a little on the skinny side for me. I'm going to fatten you up."

The children were terrified. Gretel could only do what the old

28

witch told her to do, and Hansel was locked in the cage day and night, and the witch kept a close eye on the only key to it.

Every morning the old witch went to the cage and told Hansel to put out his finger so she could feel how fat he was. But fortunately witches do not have very good eyesight and each morning, instead of his finger, Hansel put out a smooth rounded stick for her to feel.

"Bah!" she cried. "All your sister's lovely cooking and you're just skin and bone."

Gretel was made to prepare more food for her brother to eat and then had to clean the cottage from top to bottom, and she found all sorts of treasure boxes of gold and jewels!

The witch was growing impatient.

"I've waited long enough," she said to Hansel one day. "You should be fat by now. Gretel can get the big oven burning, and I will cook you tomorrow."

By noon the next day a pan was bubbling furiously on the hob, and the oven was alight.

"Check the oven," the witch told Gretel, planning to push her in and eat her too.

"But how will I know if it is hot enough?" said Gretel.

"Just put your head inside, you silly girl," replied the witch.

"But I don't think it will fit," said the little girl.

"Oh, just let me do it," shouted the old witch impatiently. "Get out of my way and I'll show you."

Gretel stood closely behind the witch as she bent down to look at the oven.

"Yes, yes, the temperature is just right," said the evil witch.

But before she could stand up again, clever Gretel gave her an enormous push, shoving her right into the oven, head first. Then she slammed the door tightly shut behind her and fastened it shut.

"Let me out!" shrieked the witch. "Let me out!"

"No!" yelled Gretel, running to find the key to the cage. Then she rushed to let her brother out.

They hugged each other. The witch was dead and they were free.

"Let's go home," said Hansel.

"Wait a moment," said Gretel, and she ran back into the cottage with her brother

and showed him the boxes of treasure full of gold and jewels. The children put as much as they could in their pockets and even in their shoes.

"When we get home we'll be rich," said Gretel. "Father need never work again."

The children walked for the whole day, but by evening they reached a part of the forest that they knew. Soon they were running down a familiar path.

"Father! Father!" they called, as they caught sight of the cottage. "We're home!"

Their father was working outside the cottage when he heard the children. He was very sad. He had lost his beloved children and in the last few days his wife had died too.

He looked up when he heard their voices.

"I must be dreaming," he said, and then he saw them. He was so happy to have them home again.

"I'll never, never send you away again," he told them, as he hugged them.

"Everything will be alright," said Gretel, and she and Hansel emptied their pockets. With all the jewels, they would never be hungry again.

LITTLE
RED RIDING HOOD

Once upon a time, there was a little girl who lived with her parents in a cottage on the edge of the forest. Her father was a woodcutter. He worked all day long in the forest, chopping down trees with his huge axe.

Right in the middle of the forest was another sweet little cottage. It belonged to the little girl's grandmother.

The kind old lady loved her granddaughter very much and, one day, decided to make her a present. It was a red cloak with a red hood to match.

The cloak looked so nice that the little girl wore it all the time. And that is why

35

everybody called her Red Riding Hood.

One day Grandmother fell ill, so Red Riding Hood's mother baked her a cake and made her some fresh butter, just to make her feel better.

"Red Riding Hood," called her mother. "Take this cake and butter to Grandmother's cottage. A visit from you will cheer her up!"

So Red Riding Hood picked up the basket, waved goodbye to her mother and went off down the path.

She hadn't gone very far when she met a wolf. He trotted up, pretending to be friendly. "Good morning, Red Riding Hood. What have you got in your basket today?"

"I have some fresh butter and a cake,"

replied the little girl. "They are for my grandmother, who lives in the middle of the forest. She is ill and needs cheering up."

The wolf licked his lips. 'How I would love to gobble up this little girl. But if I am clever, I can eat her grandmother as well,' he sniggered.

"Red Riding Hood," said the wolf slyly. "We will both go to visit your grandmother and cheer her up. I'll race you there!"

Then the clever wolf said to Red Riding Hood, "You follow this path and I will find another one. Then we'll see who reaches Grandmother's cottage first!"

Red Riding Hood was a sweet and trusting little girl and agreed that this would be fun. No sooner was the little girl out of sight, than the wicked wolf ran off at top speed.

As for Red Riding Hood, she wandered slowly along the path picking flowers and wild strawberries for her grandmother. She had forgotten all about the race.

That wicked wolf knew every secret path and short cut in the forest. He ran so fast, the animals and birds didn't even notice him.

Quietly he crept round a clearing in the trees where the woodcutter was chopping wood. On and on he raced until he came to the middle of the forest.

The wolf reached Grandmother's cottage in next to no time. He ran up the path and knocked on the door.

"Who is that?" cried Grandmother from her bed.

"It is only me, Red Riding Hood," replied the wolf, in

his softest voice.

"Lift the latch and come right in," the old lady called. "The door isn't locked, my dear."

The wolf bounded in and gobbled up poor Grandmother whole!

"That was delicious," sighed the wicked wolf, smacking his lips. "Now for Red Riding Hood!"

The wolf looked around the bedroom. He found one of Grandmother's spare night-

dresses and her nightcap, so he put them on as fast as he could, and then pulled the curtains closed to darken the room. Then he jumped into bed and waited for Red Riding Hood.

At last the little girl reached the cottage door and tapped very gently.

"Who is it?" asked the wolf, trying to sound like Grandmother.

"It's Red Riding Hood. I've bought you some cake and fresh butter."

The wolf grinned. "Lift the latch and walk right in," he croaked. So Red Riding Hood opened the door and came inside.

"You sound very strange," called Red Riding Hood.

"I have a cold, my dear!" the wolf replied. "Come here, so that I can see you."

Little Red Riding Hood's eyes slowly adjusted to the darkened room. She was shocked when she saw her grandmother. "Why, Grandmother, what strong arms you have!" she said.

"All the better to hug you with!" replied the wolf.

"Why, Grandmother, what big ears you have!" said Red Riding Hood.

"All the better to hear you with!" the wolf cried.

"Why, Grandmother, what big eyes you have!" said Red Riding Hood, staring at him.

"All the better to see you with!" the wolf grinned.

"Why, Grandmother, what big teeth you have!" gasped Red

Riding Hood.

"All the better to EAT you with!" snarled the wolf. And with that, he threw back the bedclothes and leapt out of bed. Poor Red Riding Hood screamed at the top of her voice as the wolf tried to grab her and gobble her up. She escaped from the bedroom and dashed out of the house, the hungry wolf close behind!

Now Red Riding Hood's father was chopping wood nearby and he heard the little girl's screams.

He grabbed his huge axe and ran towards the cottage. He saw the wolf chasing Red Riding Hood and guessed what had happened. The brave woodcutter raised his axe and chopped the wolf in two with one blow. The wolf fell dead and Red Riding

Hood was saved.

The frightened little girl ran to her father and kissed and hugged him.

But what a surprise they got when they turned round ... there stood Grandmother safe and sound! Because the woodcutter had chopped the wolf in two, Grandmother was able to climb out quite unharmed.

So all three went back inside the cottage. They unpacked the basket Red Riding

Hood had brought and ate the delicious cake.

Little Red Riding Hood never again went walking in the forest alone, and Grandmother took great care to lock her cottage door.